THE SECRET MAGIC OF
FOOTBALL

By Mia Wilson
Illustrations by Ugur Kose

This is a work of fiction. Names, characters, places, and incidents either are the product of the author's imagination or are used fictitiously. Any resemblance to actual persons, living or dead, events, or locales is entirely coincidental.

Copyright © 2025 Oldbird Publishing

All rights reserved. No part of this book may be reproduced or used in any manner without written permission of the copyright owner except for the use of quotations in a book review.

For more information, email fiona@oldbirdpublishing.com

First paperback edition August 2025

Story by Mia Wilson

Illustrations by Ugur Kose

ISBN 978-1-7392-6879-4 (paperback)

www.oldbirdpublishing.com

CONTENTS

1 THE DREAM LEAGUE

Once upon a time in Kirkcaldy, two brothers, Finlay and Brodie, shared a dream as big as the Fife skies above them. Both devoted fans of the town's beloved football team, Raith Rovers, the boys promised each other they'd play for them one day.

Every weekend, they joined their dad at Stark's Park, cheering on the players as they gave their all on the pitch. One dark October evening, after another thrilling match where Raith Rovers scored a last-minute goal to secure victory, Finlay and Brodie lay under a blanket fort in their room. They were talking about their grandest dream—to one day play for Raith Rovers themselves.

"Imagine wearing the Rovers blue, Finlay," Brodie said, his eyes shining. "Scoring the winning goal in front of the whole stadium!"

Finlay grinned. "And hearing the crowd chant our names! Brodie! Finlay! Rovers legends!"

That night, as the boys talked about how cool playing for the Rovers would be and moonlight streamed through their bedroom window, something extraordinary happened. The large Raith Rovers poster on their bedroom wall began to emit a soft glow in the darkness, surprising the sleepy brothers. The room suddenly filled with a bright light as a strong yank dragged them towards the poster. Like water swirling down a drain, they suddenly found themselves whirling, whirling, until they finally landed on the lush green pitch of Stark's Park, wearing Raith Rovers jerseys with their names emblazoned on the back!

"What's happening?" said Brodie, barely audible, clutching his brother's arm.

A voice rang out from the stands. "Welcome, young Rovers! Your team needs you!" Captain McNaught, the legendary Raith Rovers player from years past, made his way toward them.

"The Dream League is in danger," McNaught announced. "Only those with real passion for the game can save it. You've got to face the Shadow Squad, a team built on fear and doubt. If they win, the joy of football will vanish from Kirkcaldy for good."

Finlay and Brodie exchanged resolute looks. "We're ready," they chimed in unison.

With a whistle, the game began. The Shadow Squad was agile and wily, but Finlay and Brodie gave it their all. Time and again, Brodie weaved through the Shadow Squad's defence, while Finlay's powerful shots tested their goalkeeper over and over. The stands, filled with dream-like figures of past and present fans, including their dad, erupted in cheers!

Rovers had won!

The stands roared with excitement, and Captain McNaught approached the boys. "You've saved the spirit of football in Kirkcaldy, lads. Never forget, it's not just about winning; it's about playing with determination and bringing the community together."

Before the boys could respond, with an almighty whoosh, they found themselves back in their beds. The sparkling poster dimmed, now showing Finlay and Brodie standing proudly on the pitch, their dream moment captured forever.

"Was...was that real?" Brodie stuttered, wide-eyed.

"I think so." Finlay beamed. "And I think we're one step closer to our dream."

As they eventually drifted off to sleep, the distant sound of cheering fans seemed to echo through the night, a reminder that dreams and football magic are always within reach.

2 FINAL WHISTLE

In the historic town of Kirkcaldy, where the waves of the Firth of Forth lapped against the sandy shores, lived a boy named Paul. Every weekend during the football season, he donned his navy-and-white scarf and headed to the stadium to watch Raith Rovers and cheer on his home team. He loved the excitement of the matches and dreamed of being part of it, but he was unlike many of his school pals who wished to score the winning goal in the Scottish Cup Final. No, Paul had a different dream: he wanted to become a football referee! With their sharp whistles and watchful eyes, they ran the game with fairness and authority.

"I'll be the best referee Scotland's ever seen," Paul declared one morning at school, his eyes gleaming.

His careers teacher, Mr Ferguson, scoffed when he overheard Paul's announcement. "You? A referee? You can't even answer when called on in class. You need confidence to make decisions on the pitch—aim for a job you can actually do!"

Paul's cheeks burned, and his heart sank a little, but he was not one to give up easily. That evening as he sat with his granddad, a former groundsman at the club, Paul told him about Mr Ferguson's comments.

Granddad chuckled, his eyes twinkling. "Paul, you don't have to be loud to be a referee. The most important thing is they are firm and ensure the game is played fair and square. If it's your dream, don't let anyone steer you away from it."

Encouraged by his granddad's words, Paul decided to prove just how serious he was about his dream. He borrowed an old whistle his granddad had kept from his days working at Stark's Park.

"This whistle has seen some great games," Granddad said as he handed it over. "Maybe it'll bring you a little luck."

Paul scurried down to the Beveridge Park, where he usually went in his free time to watch his friends play football. He gripped the whistle tight in his fist. When he arrived, his friend Seb called him over to the group, asking if he wanted to keep score like usual. He stood in front of the players and noticed the whistle growing warm in his hand. He felt a strange sense of calm and focus, as if it carried the wisdom of every match it had overseen. It wasn't flashy or mysterious—just a quiet presence that seemed to offer to guide him.

"No," Paul stated firmly, surprising Seb and the others gathered. "I'll be the referee today."

From then on, Paul always played with his friends in the Beveridge Park, confidently calling out fouls and offsides. He studied the rules of football until he knew them by heart. He even practised running backwards, just like the referees did on TV.

One day, Stark's Park held a special event: a kids' mini-football match during halftime at a Raith Rovers game. Paul volunteered to referee. With his granddad's whistle in hand, his heart raced as the game began.

"Offside!" Paul called confidently, halting play. The crowd cheered as they realised he'd got the call spot on.

Mr Ferguson was in the stands that day, and even he looked impressed. After the match, the real referee, a towering man named Mr Mackie, approached Paul.

"You've got a keen eye, lad," he said with a smile. "Keep at it, and you might find yourself refereeing in the Premiership one day."

From that moment, Paul knew he could achieve his dream. The whistle became his companion, a small but steady reminder of his purpose. Though Mr Ferguson never became his biggest supporter, Paul didn't mind. He had his granddad, Seb, and even Mr Mackie cheering him on. And though he couldn't explain it, he often felt like the whistle was humming softly, as if it, too, were dreaming of the games yet to come.

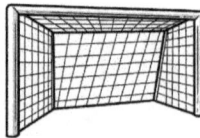

3 OLIVIA'S BIG GOAL

Olivia sat on the floor, her knees tucked under her chin as she quickly tied on her favourite football boots, their leather now heavily scuffed and worn from hours of practice. She double knotted the laces, then rushed out the door, shouting "Bye!" to her mum as she hurried to the park. Olivia loved football more than anything in the world, but her dreams of playing for Raith Rovers Women and Girls FC felt as far away as the stars at night.

At school, the boys teased her relentlessly. "You're too small," they would jeer. "You'd get blown over by the wind!"

But Olivia didn't care. Every day after school and her chores were done, she'd head to the Beveridge Park with her football where she could practice in secret, far away from the jeers and mocking of the boys in her class. The uneven grass became her stadium, and the rusty swings her cheering crowd. She practised dribbling, shooting, and passing, and though she was told she was too short to be competitive, she worked until her legs ached and the sun dipped below the horizon.

That evening, she practised just like always, until she could play no more. As Olivia sat catching her breath under a tree, the faintest of lights glinted at the corner of her eye. Startled, she turned to see a tiny figure—a glowing, winged fairy no taller than her hand.

17

"Hello," the fairy said in a voice as light as a whisper. "I am Isabella, the Keeper of Dreams. I've seen your heart, Olivia, and I'm here to help."

Olivia blinked, sure she was imagining things. "Help with what?"

"With what you already have," Isabella replied, pointing to the battered and worn football boots on Olivia's feet. She fluttered close and touched them lightly. They glimmered briefly, then returned to normal. "I've put a charm on your boots," Isabella said. "But remember, the spell only works when you believe in yourself."

Before she could reply, the fairy vanished, leaving behind a dazed and confused Olivia. Did that really happen? Was she dreaming...had she dozed off under the tree?

The next day at school, Olivia saw a flyer pinned to the P.E. notice board.

"Raith Rovers Girls Open Under-15s Trials: This Saturday at 10 AM."

Her heart skipped a beat. This was her chance! But when she told her friends, some boys overheard, and the teasing grew worse.

"You? Try out for Raith Rovers?" laughed Jake, the tallest and loudest boy. "They'll need a magnifying glass just to find you on the pitch!"

Olivia's cheeks burned, but she refused to let his words sink her hopes. That evening, she told her dad about the trials. "Well," he said with a warm smile, "Raith Rovers would be lucky to have someone as determined as you. Let's practice together tomorrow."

And they did. Olivia's dad set up cones in the garden for dribbling drills. He told her to weave between the cones, keeping the ball just in front. Olivia's chest was tight as she started running around, the ball rolling swiftly ahead. She'd never been so light on her feet! Her shooting never more accurate! She looked down, smiling, at the blur her feet became as she rushed around on the grass.

"You've got quick feet, Olivia," her father praised. "Use that to your advantage."

When Saturday arrived, her mum surprised her with some brand-new football boots that Olivia had requested for her upcoming birthday. "These will show off those quick feet!" chirped Mum happily. Oh, no! What could Olivia do? Her old boots were battered, true enough, and a tad too small, but what about the charm? As Mum whisked the old ones away, Olivia's heart sank as she realised she had no choice but to wear the new boots.

Olivia's stomach was in knots with nerves. The trials were held on a proper pitch, surrounded by players older and much taller than her, plus she wasn't wearing her charmed boots!

The coach blew his whistle and called the girls together, telling them to line up as he explained the drills that were next up in the trials. The drills were tough. Olivia had to weave between cones, pass the ball with precision, and shoot into a small goal, but she kept stumbling, her legs twisting beneath her. The first two times she came up to the goal, she tripped right over the ball! She could feel her dream running away from her, just out of reach. But she remembered her dad's advice—and the fairy's words.

Next, the girls were split into teams. At first, she struggled to keep up with the taller players. But when she got a touch of the ball, she felt in control, as if it knew exactly where she wanted it to go.

Her size seemed to make the coaches hesitate initially, but something changed as she moved. Her speed and skill began to shine. She darted past defenders during the practice match, scoring a goal that left even the coaches clapping. She noticed the ball almost seemed to glide along with her, responding perfectly to her every touch.

At the end of the trial, one of the coaches called her name. "Olivia, you've got incredible talent. Welcome to Raith Rovers."

Olivia's heart soared. She couldn't wait to tell her mum and dad and even the teasing boys at school. She had proven that dreams weren't about size or charmed boots but heart and belief.

Olivia drifted to sleep that night, her new football boots sitting neatly by her bed. Briefly, a faint light glowed once more beside her sleeping head. In her dreams, Isabella appeared for a second time, her voice a gentle whisper. "The skill was in you all along, Olivia. The boots just enabled you to see it."

From that night on, Olivia knew that no dream was too big when chased with courage, hard work, and a little sprinkle of fairy dust.

THE MATCHDAY PROGRAMME

Whenever the family came to visit, Christopher's grandfather would sit him in front of the TV and turn on the Raith Rovers game, no matter who they were playing. His grandfather loved the team, and, though Christopher loved his grandfather, he just could never get into football the way he seemed to want him to. What Christopher loved the most about visiting was his grandfather's huge house, especially the attic. It was a treasure trove of memories, with boxes full of forgotten wonders. One blustery afternoon, as the wind rattled the windows and his grandfather cheered on the Rovers, Christopher climbed the creaky stairs with his torch in hand, ready for another adventure.

He sifted through boxes marked Old Books, Family Photos, and Miscellaneous, until one caught his eye—Raith Rovers. Intrigued, he opened it to find a jumble of scarves, badges, and faded match programmes. Right at the bottom was one dated June 6, 1968. The cover showed an old Stark's Park, its colours faded. As Christopher picked it up, the paper shifted in his hands as if it had a life of its own.

Then the attic spun. Christopher reached for something, anything, to stop the spinning, but there was nothing but wind lifting him up and rushing between his fingers, whipping against his face, until his feet suddenly scraped against solid ground again, and the spinning stopped. The air filled with distant cheers, growing louder and louder. Before he could process what was happening, Christopher was no longer in the attic but standing outside Stark's Park.

Around him, fans in vintage clothes waved flags and queued for tickets. A boy about Christopher's age stood nearby, fiddling with a small transistor radio. He had curly hair and an easygoing air.

"First match?" the boy asked.

Christopher hesitated, his mind reeling. "Uh…yeah."

"Don't worry," the boy said with a laugh, slapping Christopher on the back. "You're in for a treat. Name's Rennie."

"I'm Christopher," he replied, still dazed.

"Stick with me," Rennie said. "I've got the best spot."

The stadium was buzzing. Fans filled the stands, their voices a mix of chants and laughter. The players warmed up on the field, their boots thudding softly on the grass. Christopher followed Rennie to a spot near the front, near the action.

"This," Rennie said, spreading his arms, "is Stark's Park. Best place in the world."

Christopher wasn't sure he agreed—football had never been his thing—but something about Rennie's enthusiasm made him smile.

"Why do you love it so much?" Christopher asked.

Rennie grinned. "It's the feeling that you belong."

As the match began, it was impossible to not be swept up in the excitement. He cheered, gasped, and groaned along with Rennie. The players moved like heroes on a battlefield, pressing forward purposefully. All around him, the crowd swelled with excitement, jumping and cheering and moving as one.

At halftime, his new friend turned to him. "So? What do you think?"

Christopher laughed. "It's…brilliant. I get it now."

"Told you," Rennie said, his grin wide. "Football's like that. It's magic when you let it in."

When the final whistle blew, the crowds in the stands roared with delight. Christopher felt connected to it all—the fans, the game, the history.

"You'll remember this day," Rennie murmured, his voice becoming faint. "Trust me."

The world around Christopher blurred. The crowd's noise faded, and Stark's Park's colours melted away.

When he opened his eyes, he was back in the attic, holding the programme. The cheers still echoed faintly in his ears.

He bolted downstairs, where his grandfather was dozing on the sofa. "Granddad, do you remember this game?" he asked, thrusting the programme into his hands.

His grandfather's eyes lit up as he reached for his glasses. "June 6, 1968. Aye, I was there. One of the best matches I've ever seen. I was just a lad, standing in the crowd."

"Were you...were you called Rennie back then?" Christopher asked hesitantly.

His grandfather chuckled. "Rennie? Gosh, it's a long time since I've heard that. Aye, that was my nickname. Well, having the surname Macintosh like the Scottish architect, of course, and the lads always had a way with names. Believe me, others were called a lot worse! Why do you ask?"

Christopher caught his breath sharply. The realisation hit him like a tidal wave. He'd met his grandfather as a boy and stood in the stands amid the roar of the crowd as they treasured the magic of Stark's Park. He finally saw the game in a whole new way—through his beloved grandfather's eyes.

5. THE WINNING KIT

Once upon a time, in a quiet village, there lived a boy named Archie. His village was small, with few children the same age as him, so he spent a lot of time entertaining himself. He was a kind and creative soul with a love for watching football that was only rivalled by his passion for art and sewing. When most of his school pals in Kirkcaldy were out practising their free kicks and debating their favourite players, Archie was inside the cosy cottage he shared with his dad and younger brother, drawing elaborate sketches and designing patterns.

At school, Art & Design and Home Economics were his favourite subjects. While others might grumble about still life painting or sewing a Christmas tree decoration, Archie thrived, his mind always buzzing with ideas. He dreamed of designing something extraordinary one day, even if many of the boys teased him for liking things they thought were "just for girls."

"Hey, Archie," one of them sniggered during lunch. "Why don't you knit us some scarves for the next match?" Archie would just shrug.

"Maybe I will. You'll need them when Raith wins in the winter!"

Despite the teasing, Archie never let their words crush his creativity. Whenever classmates would make fun of him, he just turned to his hobbies—he would sew and paint and bake, finding happiness in the activities he loved.

One day, an announcement was made in the school bulletin, which Archie's teacher read to the class.

"Wow, look at this, folks! Raith Rovers Football Club is running a competition to design their new away kit! The winning design will be worn by the team next season. Isn't that amazing?"

Archie sat bolt upright. Was this for real? A chance to combine his two big passions, football and design? But he couldn't tell his classmates of his plans...they would make fun of him. Still, Archie was tenacious.

That evening, he went straight to work, his mind racing with ideas. But as Archie sat at the dining table, with sketches and material samples spread out before him, nothing seemed to work. Either the pattern looked bland or the colours were wrong or the shape was too strange. He started to worry— maybe he wasn't good enough. The thought made his throat tighten and his eyes burn, making it hard to do the very thing he loved the most! Until suddenly, he heard a soft sound, like the rustle of fabric in the wind. Startled, he looked up. On the table's edge sat an old pair of scissors, ones he'd found in a dusty corner of the school's Home Economics cupboard.

Archie hesitated, then picked them up. Their handles were wrapped in soft leather, and the blades seemed to vibrate with a faint warmth. The scissors fit perfectly in his hand as if they had been waiting for this moment. With every cut he made, the fabric seemed to take on a life of its own, lying perfectly flat, edges clean and precise. It wasn't flashy or obvious magic—just the quiet kind that makes everything feel like it's going exactly as it should.

Archie wanted the kit to reflect the essence of his favourite team—a blend of tradition and modern flair. He added blue and red vertical stripes, a nod to the club's history, with a bold yellow chevron across the chest for a stylish splash of colour. He neatly stitched a small thistle emblem on the back collar, symbolising Scottish pride.

For days, Archie worked tirelessly, the scissors always within reach. He stayed up late sketching, stitching, and testing fabrics from the sewing supplies his Home Economics teacher had kindly provided. He started eating his tea while hunched over his project, working till his fingers ached and he could barely hold a needle, his eyes blurring till he couldn't follow his own pattern. When he finally submitted his design, Archie was excited, exhausted, and unsure of what to expect next.

A month passed, and Archie had started to give up hope. He went about his days as usual—school, assisting with costumes for the school play, helping his dad in the kitchen—but waiting for the result of the competition weighed heavy on him. Finally, during a school assembly, the headteacher announced, "Congratulations to Archie Murrey here at Balwearie High School. His design has been chosen as the new away kit for Raith Rovers!"

Applause thundered across the assembly hall. Even the boys who had teased Archie were gobsmacked. When Archie went up to accept his prize—a stunning framed version of his winning jersey—his head was held high.

On the first day the team wore his kit at an away match, Archie and his family sat in the stands as guests of honour. The players looked sharp, and the fans loved the design. Archie noticed the tiniest detail; the thistle on the collar seemed to catch the breeze in a way that made it stand out like it had its own quiet strength.

The boys at school never teased him again. Instead, they asked him for ideas for match posters and respected Archie's opinions on their outfits. From then on, Archie knew being true to himself was worth every challenge. He had proven that the quietest tools and true dedication could sometimes create the most dazzling victories.

Archie kept the scissors in a small box on his bedroom desk, a reminder of that special project. And though he never spoke about it, he often felt they were waiting, ready for the next time he needed a little extra help creating something extra special.

THE SECRET OF THE MIDNIGHT MATCH

Max was an adventurous girl who loved sport, and football more than anything. She loved to practise in the park with her friends, dreaming of becoming a star player. But what intrigued her most were the rumours about the midnight match at Stark's Park. She'd heard mention of it from her parents, of course, and her older brother even claimed to have seen the lights once when he was younger!

She begged her brother to tell her more details until she finally bothered him so much, he gave in. The football pitch at Stark's Park seemed ordinary during the day. But something secret happened when the clock struck midnight on the night of a full moon. The pitch would light up on its own, bathed in a soft, silvery aura, and mysterious players would appear as if from nowhere.

"This story has been told to Kirkcaldy children for decades," her brother said. "No one knows who these players are, and no fan has ever seen the game. Not even me."

Max, believing she was the biggest fan of all, decided she would find out.

That very evening was a full moon, and, determined to solve the mystery, Max packed a blanket and torch, waited until her family were asleep, then slipped out the back door and rode her bike to the stadium.

The moon hung proudly in the sky, casting long shadows as Max reached the gates. She quickly hid her bike and scrambled over the wall, trying not to make a sound as she landed heavily on the other side.

The place was dark and spooky at night, but Max was undaunted. At first, nothing happened. The pitch was silent, and she started to think the stories might just be legends. But as the clock struck midnight, the air grew still. Suddenly, a faint hum filled the air, and the grass quivered, emitting the gentlest silver light! One by one, glowing figures emerged from the shadows, one carrying a ball that sparkled like stardust.

Max's heart raced. It was true! Her throat was dry and tight, but she couldn't resist—she stepped out from her hiding spot. "H-hello?" she called hesitantly.

The strangely illuminated players gently turned towards her, their faces kind but unfamiliar. One of them, a tall figure wearing a captain's armband, stepped forward. "Welcome, Max," he said in a voice that seemed to echo softly. "We've been waiting for you."

She blinked in surprise. "You know who I am?"

The captain nodded. "Of course. We're the Guardians of the Game. We once played the greatest matches under this very moon. When our time ended, we vowed to keep playing, waiting for someone with true dedication to join us. That someone is you."

Max could hardly believe it. "Me? But I'm just a kid!"

The captain smiled. "A true player isn't measured by experience, but by their love for the game. Will you play?" Max's heart thumped in her chest. "Yes!" she exclaimed, dropping her bag at the edge of the pitch and darting after him.

The Guardians split into two teams, and the game began. The ball sparkled as it zipped across the field, leaving trails of lights in its wake. Max felt exhilarated, weaving through defenders and delivering sharp, precise passes like never before.

Throughout the match, the Guardians guided her with encouraging words.

"Trust your instincts," one called out as she prepared for a shot.

"Play with joy," another said as she dashed toward the goal. "Remember why you love this game!"

With the match drawing to a close, the score was tied. Seconds remained when the ball landed at Max's feet. Suddenly, she felt dizzy and everything seemed to tilt sideways, she couldn't get her legs to move! Then, remembering the advice of the Guardians, she took one deep breath, then another. Everything straightened out and sharpened into focus. With a swift kick, she sent the ball curving into the top corner of the net.

The players cheered loudly, and the sparkling light of the ball brightened for a moment before fading. The game was over, and the Guardians gathered around her.

"You've proven yourself, Max," the captain said. "Remember, the heart of the game isn't just about scoring goals or being a star player—it's about teamwork and bringing people together. Share that with others."

Before she could reply, the Guardians began to fade, their figures dissolving into the moonlight. The pitch returned to its usual state, quiet and still. Max stood there, her mind racing, but she was happy. She knew what she had to do.

She never told anyone exactly what happened that night at Stark's Park, but from then on, Max's love for the game grew even stronger. Every time she played, she carried the lessons of the midnight match with her—to trust, to play with joy, and to always keep the game's true essence alive.

PHANTOM GOALKEEPER

An old football field lay on the edge of Kirkcaldy, nestled between tall trees and whistling winds. It wasn't much to look at—the goalposts were rusted, the nets torn, the goalmouth muddy and grassless—but for Greg and his friends, it was their favourite place in the world. Every evening, when the light allowed, they gathered for a game. While his friends were full of dreams of becoming strikers and forwards, earning points to win the toughest of games, Greg dreamed of being Scotland's greatest goalkeeper!

One cool autumn afternoon, Greg and his friends played their usual match. The game lasted way longer than usual, to the point that the sun had dipped below the horizon, leaving the sky painted in hues of orange and red. Greg's side was leading 1-0 with seconds to go, but an opponent was lining up for a final shot at the goal.

The player scuffed the ball, and it was obvious it was going to miss. Greg felt himself relax slightly when a sudden gust of wind swept through the field, sending the ball veering back on course. But instead of flying into the goal, it stopped mid-air and then sailed straight past the ragged net.

Everyone froze.

"D-did you see that?" gasped Greg's best friend, Calum.

"No one touched it," whimpered another teammate, eyes wide.

The kids exchanged nervous glances. "Maybe it's...a phantom goalkeeper!" Calum joked, trying to lighten the mood. But his voice wavered, and no one laughed.

It was getting late, so his friends gathered their things and started jostling each other as they got ready to head home, but Greg's curiosity got the better of him. He wondered what was going on, so he took his time as he wrapped up his boots and packed his bag, stretching it out until he was waving at his friends to head off without him. He shouted bye as they left the field, and he turned back to his bag, hands shaking as he zipped it closed. The field was quiet, and the cool night air wrapped around him like a blanket that made him shiver. Just as he was about to give up and go home, he heard it— the faint sound of a ball bouncing. Greg's breath caught in his throat.

"Who's there?" he called, his voice trembling.

A figure emerged from the shadows near the goal. It was faint and rippling, like a reflection on water. The figure wore an old-fashioned goalkeeper's jersey, gloves, and boots with nailed-on leather studs.

"Who are you?" Greg asked, his fear giving way to curiosity. The figure's voice was soft but clear.

"I am James, a goalkeeper here long ago. They called me The Wall, for no ball could get past me. I made so many amazing saves in my time, but I always felt like I still had even more to give. I've stayed here ever since, hoping for one more chance to prove myself."

Greg's fear melted completely. "You were amazing tonight. That save...it was incredible. Why don't you join our games?"

James smiled sadly. "I cannot. Touching real things is very difficult; pushing the ball away today took most of my energy. But perhaps, if you're willing, I can teach you everything I know about goalkeeping?"

From that night on, Greg would sneak back to the field after dark. James taught him the secrets of goalkeeping—how to read an opponent's movements, dive with perfect timing, and stay calm under pressure. Greg listened intently, practising until his hands were sore and his legs ached.

One day, Greg's school team faced their biggest rival in a local tournament. The opposing team was known for their powerful strikers, and Greg's teammates were nervous. But Greg, now a vastly improved goalkeeper thanks to James's lessons, felt ready.

The match was intense, and the score was 1 - 0 as the final seconds ticked away. Greg was tense but ready. His heart beat steadily, and his breaths were deep; James had taught him well, and he had nothing to worry about. The rival team's best player charged toward the goal, his eyes blazing with determination. He kicked the ball with all his might. Greg leapt, stretching as far as he could, and caught the ball mid-air.

The crowd went wild—Greg's team had won! As his friends surrounded him, celebrating, Greg glanced to his left. For a moment, he thought he saw James standing beside the goal, smiling proudly before fading into the evening mist.

As the years passed, Greg grew stronger, quicker, and more skilled with each passing season. He defended his school team through every match, then his first club, Raith Rovers, after being scouted. Finally, he was called up to play for Scotland's national team. As he stood between the posts for his country, no matter how intense the pressure was, Greg heard only James, whispering, "Trust yourself, Greg. You're ready."

A MAGIC MATCH

Stark's Park, home of Raith Rovers, sat high in the Kirkcaldy skyline. On game days, the town would flood the streets leading up to the ground, the crowd humming with excitement as they slowly filed into the stadium. Young Amrit was a fixture in the stands every weekend, cheering his heart out alongside his dad. But one drizzly Friday evening, an unusual meeting took place—something he would remember forever.

After watching the team's practice, Amrit left the training ground and noticed an old, white-bearded man sitting near the gates. He had a woolly hat in Raith Rovers' colours perched on his head and an odd glint in his eye.

"Evening, lad," the man said with a kind smile. "I see you've got the spirit of Raith Rovers in you."

Amrit puffed out his chest. "I love Raith Rovers! One day, I'm going to play for them."

The old man chuckled. "Excellent! But tell me, how would you like to help the team right now?"

"Help? Me?" the boy replied, wide-eyed.

The old man leaned in and spoke softly. "The team has been struggling, eh? Losing some games, low on confidence? But I have something that might just bring them luck." He pulled a beautiful Mitre Delta football from a shabby, plastic carrier bag at his feet. The leather had an unusual lustre that seemed to change colour as the old man held the ball out towards Amrit. "This here is the Magic Match Ball. When used with true belief, it can inspire greatness—but only for those who play with heart."

Amrit's mouth fell open. "Magic? Really?"

"Aye," the man said, passing the ball to the boy. "See how it feels when your fingers touch it? But remember, it's not the ball that wins the game—it's the players. The magic just helps bring out their best. Now, off you go, lad. Make sure the team gets it tomorrow."

"But why me? Can't you bring it to them?"

"It has to be you," the old man said. "I'm too old; I'd never make it down. But I've seen you running around the stadium for years—you know it better than anyone. You can find a way onto the pitch."

Amrit took the ball and held it close, nodding to the man. He raced home, his heart pounding. That night, he could barely sleep, the ball safely tucked at the foot of his bed.

The next day, the rain clouds had cleared, and Stark's Park was buzzing with fans. Raith Rovers were set to play their biggest rivals, Dunfermline Athletic. Amrit told his dad he was going to buy a drink, slipping from his seat with the ball under his arm. He headed toward the food stalls but, glancing back at his dad, darted the other way. He scurried down halls and stairs, tucking himself behind corners and bins to avoid being spotted, before finally making it round to near the dugout. He hopped over the barrier to the pitch to the sound of surprised yells and raced toward where the players were warming up.

"Excuse me!" he called out as he sprinted up to his favourite player, John Baird. "I've got something that can help us win!" He stopped abruptly before the striker, thrusting the ball towards him with outstretched arms.

With a friendly smile, John crouched down to speak to Amrit. "What's this, lad? A lucky charm?" the player asked with a curious grin, noticing the silky, lustrous leather.

"It's magic!" Amrit said excitedly. "It'll help you play your best—but only if you believe in yourselves."

John let out a soft chuckle but paused when he caught the hopeful look in the young boy's eyes. He nodded seriously.

"Alright, lad. Let's see what it can do."

As the game kicked off, something remarkable began to unfold. Each time a player got a touch of the ball, they seemed faster, their passes crisper, and their movements almost perfectly coordinated. The crowd noticed, too, murmurs of amazement rippling through the stadium—something special was happening on the pitch.

"Look at them go!" someone shouted from the stands.

But despite how amazingly the team was playing, by halftime, the game was tied 1-1. The crowd was on edge, and the electric atmosphere in the stadium made Amrit's heart pound with anticipation.

When the second half started, Dunfermline came thundering out, nearly scoring a goal. The tension among the Raith fans grew, and Amrit worried the magic might not be enough.

Then he remembered the old man's words: It's not the ball that wins the game—it's the players.

"Believe in yourselves!" Amrit yelled from the stands, his voice ringing out loud and clear.

The players seemed to hear him. The team dug deep, playing together like their opponents didn't exist. In the final seconds, John Baird made a bold, charging run and unleashed a breathtaking shot that soared into the net, clinching victory for Raith Rovers.

The crowd let out an ecstatic roar. Fans leapt to their feet, singing, waving their scarves, and chanting the team's name with uncontainable joy.

After the match, John spotted Amrit waiting by the gates. With a smile, the player approached him and handed back the gift.

"Thank you, Amrit," John said. "I'm sorry we couldn't use it, but I really appreciate your offering your special ball to us and being such a great fan."

"Wha-what?" stuttered Amrit. "You didn't use this ball?"

"No, unfortunately, the SPFL provides the match ball; it's just the rules we must follow. But I left yours in the dugout as a lucky mascot. And we played a magic game today, didn't we? I think it was the belief you had in us that gave us belief in ourselves."

Amrit beamed with pride. "I'll always believe in Raith Rovers!" Setting off for home, the boy noticed the old man watching from a distance. The man gave him a wink and disappeared into the crowd.

From that day on, Raith Rovers played with renewed pride, and Amrit knew he had played a special part in turning things around for the club, bringing a little bit of his own magic to the pitch.

9 THE GROUNDSMAN'S BOY

There once was a little boy named Kyle who loved two things more than anything else: his dad and football. His father was Mr MacLachlan, the groundsman for Raith Rovers, the football team they both adored. Every day after school, Kyle would rush to Stark's Park to watch him tend to the pitch.

Kyle loved watching him mow the grass into perfect stripes, mark the white lines precisely, and check every blade to ensure it was ready for match day. His dad made everything seem so important, and Kyle hung off his every word. "The pitch is the heart of the game," his dad would say. "Without it, there's no football."

But Kyle didn't know that the pitch at Stark's Park held a secret.

One evening, as the sun dipped low over the stands, Kyle noticed something strange. As his dad finished mowing, the grass seemed to shimmer, just for a moment, like it was a living thing. "Dad," he asked, "why does the pitch always look so perfect?"

Mr MacLachlan smiled, his eyes twinkling. He told his son that long ago, a kind-hearted groundsman had whispered an enchantment over the grass, promising it would always protect and guide those who truly loved the game "Because we care for it," he finished with a wink, "it cares for us, too."

As they locked up the stadium together, Kyle asked, "Do you think I could ever be part of Raith Rovers?"

"Son, being part of something isn't just about scoring goals. It's about knowing the game, working hard, and never giving up. You'll find your place." He smiled, ruffling his son's hair.

Years went by, and Kyle grew older. Though he wasn't the best player, his love for football never wavered. He studied the game, soaking in every match his dad let him watch from the stands, learning its rhythms and secrets, how to read the plays, understand tactics, and see the beauty in teamwork. When he finished at Kirkcaldy High School, Kyle wanted to stay close to football. He started coaching local youth teams, inspiring young players with his commitment and knowledge.

And whenever he had free time, he still helped his dad at Stark's Park, mowing and remarking pitch lines and checking the stability of the goal posts. Sometimes, he swore the pitch subtly encouraged him, the blades of grass bending ever so slightly to guide him.

One chilly winter morning, Kyle got a call that made his heart race. Raith Rovers needed a new assistant manager, and they'd noticed his dedication. Nervous but determined, he stepped onto the enchanted pitch. As he crossed the grass, a soft breeze suddenly brushed his cheek, filling him with a quiet confidence.

Under his leadership, the team began to thrive. Then, one day, his boss retired, and Kyle was chosen as the new manager of Raith Rovers. Standing on the sideline for his debut match, he sensed a faint, familiar warmth radiating from the ground beneath him, as though the pitch itself was rooting for him.

After a thrilling win, Kyle found his dad by the sidelines. The old groundsman smiled, his eyes glistening with pride. "You've done it, son. You've found your place—this is where you belong."

Hugging his dad, the scent of freshly cut grass brought back all those childhood memories. In that moment, he realised the truth: the magic of the pitch wasn't just in the enchantment. It was in the care, the dreams, and the love poured into it over the years.

And so, under Kyle's leadership, Raith Rovers flourished. But no matter how far he went, he always remembered the little boy who dreamed big under the floodlights of Stark's Park, guided by the quiet magic of the pitch.

About the author

Mia Wilson lives in Scotland, has two sons, and is a teacher. Her first book, Teddy Beddy Bear, is a bedtime story book for the under-3s. This is her first chapter book for older children.

About the book

This book is inspired by all Mia's friends in Kirkcaldy, and their love for Raith Rovers FC.

Did you enjoy the book?

If so, please consider giving it a review on Amazon. Reviews mean the world to independent authors.

www.ingramcontent.com/pod-product-compliance
Lightning Source LLC
LaVergne TN
LVHW091233080426
835509LV00009B/1256